The HUNDREDTH DOVE

and Other Tales

JANE YOLEN

The
HUNDREDTH DOVE

and Other Tales

Illustrated by

David Palladini

Schocken Books · New York

First published by Schocken Books 1980
10 9 8 7 6 5 4 3   87 88 89

"The Lady and the Merman," "The Hundredth Dove," and "The Maiden
Made of Fire" originally appeared in *The Magazine of Fantasy and Science
Fiction;* "The Wind Cap" and "The White Seal Maid" in *Parabola, Myth and
the Quest for Meaning.*

Library of Congress Cataloging in Publication Data
Yolen, Jane.
The hundredth dove and other tales.
Reprint of the ed. published by Crowell, New York.
CONTENTS: The hundredth dove.—The maiden made of
fire.—The wind cap. [etc.]
1. Fairy tales, American. 2. Children's stories,
American. [1. Fairy tales] I. Palladini, David.
II. Title.
[PZ8.Y78Hu 1980]   [Fic]   80–13635

Manufactured in the United States of America
Designed by Amy Hill

ISBN 0-8052-0659-0

for Michael Patrick Hearn

Contents

The HUNDREDTH DOVE

and Other Tales

THE HUNDREDTH DOVE

There once lived in the forest of old England a fowler named Hugh who supplied all the game birds for the high king's table.

The larger birds he hunted with a bow, and it was said of him that he never shot but that a bird fell, and sometimes two. But for the smaller birds that flocked like gray clouds over the forest, he used only a silken net he wove himself. This net was soft and fine and did not injure the birds though it held them fast. Then Hugh the fowler could pick and choose the plumpest of the doves for the high king's table and set the others free.

One day in early summer, Hugh was summoned to court and brought into the throne room.

Hugh bowed low, for it was not often that he was called

into the king's own presence. And indeed he felt uncomfortable in the palace, as though caught in a stone cage.

"Rise, fowler, and listen," said the king. "In one week's time I am to be married." Then, turning with a smile to the woman who sat by him, the king held out her hand to the fowler.

The fowler stared up at her. She was neat as a bird, slim and fair, with black eyes. There was a quiet in her, but a restlessness too. He had never seen anyone so beautiful.

Hugh took the tiny hand offered him and put his lips to it, but he only dared to kiss the gold ring that glittered on her finger.

The king looked carefully at the fowler and saw how he trembled. It made the king smile. "See, my lady, how your beauty turns the head of even my fowler. And he is a man who lives as solitary as a monk in his wooded cell."

The lady smiled and said nothing, but she drew her hand away from Hugh.

The king then turned again to the fowler. "In honor of my bride, the Lady Columba, whose name means dove and whose beauty is celebrated in all the world, I wish to serve one hundred of the birds at our wedding feast."

Lady Columba gasped and held up her hand. "Please do not serve them, sire."

But the king said to the fowler, "I have spoken. Do not fail me, fowler."

"As you command," said Hugh, and he bowed again. He touched his hand to his tunic, where his motto, *Servo* ("I serve"), was sewn over the heart.

Then the fowler went immediately back to the cottage deep in the forest where he lived.

There he took out the silken net and spread it upon the floor. Slowly he searched the net for snags and snarls and weakened threads. These he rewove with great care, sitting straight-backed at his wooden loom.

After a night and a day he was done. The net was as strong as his own stout heart. He laid the net down on the hearth and slept a dreamless sleep.

Before dawn Hugh set out into the forest clearing which only he knew. The trails he followed were narrower than deer runs, for the fowler needed no paths to show him the way. He knew every tree, every stone in the forest as a lover knows the form of his beloved. And he served the forest easily as well as he served the high king.

The clearing was full of life, yet so silently did the fowler move, neither bird nor insect remarked his coming. He crouched at the edge, his brown and green clothes a part of the wood. Then he waited.

A long patience was his strength, and he waited the whole of the day, neither moving nor sleeping. At dusk the doves came, settling over the clearing like a gray mist. And when they were down and greedily feeding, Hugh leaped up and swung the net over the nearest ones in a single swift motion.

He counted twenty-one doves in his net, all but one gray-blue and meaty. The last was a dove that was slim, elegant, and white as milk. Yet even as Hugh watched, the white dove slipped through the silken strands that bound it and flew away into the darkening air.

Since Hugh was not the kind of hunter to curse his bad luck, but rather one to praise his good, he gathered up the twenty and went home. He placed the doves in a large wooden cage whose bars he had carved out of white oak.

Then he looked at his net. There was not a single break in it, no way for the white dove to have escaped. Hugh thought long and hard about this, but at last he lay down to the cooing of the captured birds and slept.

In the morning the fowler was up at dawn. Again he crept to the forest clearing and waited, quieter than any stone, for the doves. And again he threw his net at dusk and caught twenty fat gray doves and the single white one.

But as before, the white dove slipped through his net as easily as air.

The fowler carried the gray doves home and caged them

with the rest. But his mind was filled with the sight of the white bird, slim and fair. He was determined to capture it.

For five days and nights it was the same except for this one thing: On the fifth night there were only nineteen gray doves in his net. He was short of the hundred by one. Yet he had taken all of the birds in the flock but the white dove.

Hugh looked into the hearth fire but he felt no warmth. He placed his hand upon the motto above his heart. "I swear by the king whom I serve and by the lady who will be his queen that I will capture that bird," he said. "I will bring the hundred doves to them. I shall not fail."

So the sixth day, well before dawn, the fowler arose. He checked the net one final time and saw it was tight. Then he was away to the clearing.

All that day Hugh sat at the clearing's edge, still as a stone. The meadow was full of life. Songbirds sang that had never sung before. Strange flowers grew and blossomed and died at his feet, yet he never looked at them. Animals that had once been and were no longer came out of the forest shadows and passed him by: the hippocampus, the gryphon, and the silken swift unicorn. But he never moved. It was for the white dove he waited, and at last she came.

In the quickening dark she floated down, feather-light and

luminous at the clearing's edge. Slowly she moved, eating and cooing and calling for her missing flock. She came in the end to where Hugh sat and began to feed at his feet.

He moved his hands once and the net was over her, then his hands were over her, too. The dove twisted and pecked but he held her close, palms upon wings, fingers on neck.

When the white dove saw she could not move, she turned her bright black eyes on the fowler and spoke to him in a cooing woman's voice.

> *"Master fowler, set me free,*
> *Gold and silver I'll give thee."*

"Neither gold nor silver tempt me," said Hugh. "*Servo* is my motto. I serve my master. And my master is the king."

Then the white dove spoke again:

> *"Master fowler, set me free,*
> *Fame and fortune follow thee."*

But the fowler shook his head and held on tight. "After the king, I serve the forest," he said. "Fame and fortune are not masters here." He rose with the white dove in his hands and made ready to return to his house.

Then the bird shook itself all over and spoke for a third time. Its voice was low and beguiling:

> *"Master fowler, free this dove,*
> *The queen will be your own true love."*

For the first time, then, though night was almost on them, the fowler noticed the golden ring that glittered and shone on the dove's foot. As if in a vision, he saw the Lady Columba again, slim and neat and fair. He heard her voice and felt her hand in his.

He began to tremble and his heart began to pulse madly. He felt a burning in his chest and limbs. Then he looked down at the dove and it seemed to be smiling at him, its black eyes glittering.

"Servo," he cried out, his voice shaking. *"Servo."* He closed his eyes and twisted the dove's neck. Then he touched the motto on his tunic. He could feel the word *Servo* impress itself coldly on his fingertips. One quick rip and the motto was torn from his breast. He flung it to the meadow floor, put the limp dove in his pouch, and went through the forest to his home.

The next day the fowler brought the hundred doves—the ninety-nine live ones and the one dead—to the king's kitchen. But there never was a wedding.

The fowler gave up hunting and lived on berries and fruit

the rest of his life. Every day he made his way to the clearing to throw out grain for the birds. Around his neck, from a chain, a gold ring glittered. And occasionally he would touch the spot on his tunic, above his heart, which was shredded and torn.

But though songbirds and sparrows ate his grain, and swallows came at his calling, he never saw another dove.

THE
MAIDEN MADE
OF FIRE

Once on the edge of a great Eastern forest there lived a charcoal burner named Ash. He was a kind of poet. Surrounded by the gray reminders of his trade, he did not see the dust. Instead he spent most of his time staring into the heart of the fire, where he saw a world of bright, fierce beauty.

And when the kiln was all burned and opened up, Ash would sit and talk to the scattered coals in rhyme as sharp and as bright as flames. The woodsmoke was intoxicating, and he was always slightly addled by its smell.

But seeing him squatting in the dust and talking to the burned-out ends of fire, the villagers thought Ash more than a little mad, a summoner of demons. And so the poor lad got himself an evil name and was friendless because of it.

Yet if he was lonely, he never talked of it. He continued to make his way through life, building his kilns like his father before him, making charcoal for the village, and talking fancies into the smoke-filled air.

One evening as he sat and stared into the heart of his fire, Ash thought he saw a maiden lying on the coals, glowing red and gold. He shook his head vigorously to shake the dream from it, but when he looked again, the girl was still there.

So he leaped up and reached into the fire, heedless of the flames that licked his wrists, and pulled the firemaid out.

She came slowly up from the coals and stood before him. Her hair hung below her shoulders in blackened wisps and her eyes were brilliant points of light. She was wrapped in nothing but smoke.

"Who are you?" whispered Ash.

The girl was silent except with her hands. And when she moved them, little tendrils of smoke hovered in the air between them.

"Who are you?" Ash asked again, louder this time.

Still the girl did not speak.

"Shall I answer for you?" he said, and when she nodded

slightly, added, "Since you are a maiden made of fire, Brenna shall be your name."

Shyly he held out his grimed hand to her, but when she moved toward him, the heat that came from her was so intense that he stepped back. Only then did he realize that his hands had been burned by the flames, and he put them behind him as if ashamed of some weakness.

"You need something to wear. You will be chilled," he said after a moment.

At that, the girl threw her head back and laughed, and her laughter was light and crackling.

Then Ash laughed too, for he realized that Brenna was not cold. Wrapped in her mantle of smoke, she was far warmer than he.

He signaled her toward him again. This time with his head, and she stepped forward suddenly. Just as suddenly she stopped and put up her hands before her, feeling the air as if it were a wall.

Looking down at the ground to see what hindered her, Ash saw the outlines of the kiln. Around the entire inside of the burned-out kiln she stepped, and was stopped again and again by a wall neither of them could see.

Brenna sank to her knees. Droplets of fire rained from

her eyes. She pointed helplessly to the coals. The embers were the borders of her world. She could not cross over.

She turned her face up at last and it was ashen and desolate. She signaled for him to come to her instead. But the charcoal burner was too afraid of her fires.

Then Ash had a thought. "I shall make you more room," he cried.

Quickly he built up little beehive-shaped kilns side by side, small fiery alcoves that burned swiftly and were soon no more than mounds of glowing coals. By night's end, he had made Brenna a palace of embers, large and rambling, where she could run like mist through the smoke-filled halls.

Brenna thanked him again and again with her brilliant smile and the tendrils of smoke she signed with her hands. And though Ash did not dare go close to her, with that smile and those thanks he was content.

For days they lived that way. Ash neglected his charcoal kilns and instead told Brenna stories and rhymes and sang her songs, which she accepted with her crackling, light laugh. He brought her little offerings: shiny leaves, smooth nuts, woven baskets, which she turned to flame with her touch. At each blaze she clapped her hands together in delight and Ash clapped with her.

In turn, Brenna danced for him, leaping high over the heaped-up coals. And she drew pictures in the dust and smoke, pictures of a fierce bright country where firebirds flew through blazing trees and incandescent flowers flared upward toward a glowing sky.

And so the days passed for them, burning out into nights filled with fiery stars.

But at last the village elders came, with their coal-black robes and their bitter mouths, to speak to Ash. They stood in a circle around him, their voices brittle and cold.

"Where is our charcoal?" one asked, his voice rising in pitch. "While you sing and dance here in the clearing, you neglect your job."

The second joined in. "Your job is to build kilns and tend the fires and set the charcoal aside for our needs. Yet for a week you have done nothing but posture before the flames and talk wild fancies into the air."

Ash tried to escape from the circle of elders, but they moved closer to him, like a tightening noose. He put his hands up in front of him and tried to explain. "I am talking to Brenna, my love, my bride."

The elders whispered to one another. "What is he saying? What does he mean?"

The oldest one silenced them with his hand. "He is quite mad. He is in love with the fire."

Ash turned round and round pleading with the circle of men. "But she is there. Can you not see her? Her hair is black and her eyes are bright and she is like a steady flame."

The oldest one spoke coldly. "There is nothing there. No girl. And no charcoal either."

"But she is there. Brenna. She is there." Ash pointed toward the embered palace. Yet even as he spoke there was doubt in his voice, and at that doubt the maiden made of fire began to fade. Slowly, like a candle guttering out, her outline wavered. She held her arms, mere outlines now, toward Ash. She sighed, and it was the sound of a fire being extinguished.

Ash looked again at the circle of villagers around him. Then back again at Brenna, who was now but a soft glow. With an effort, he thrust his doubt from him and pushed through the elders.

"Brenna," he called.

At his voice, she grew brighter, clearer. With a hand that dripped fragile tears of flame she signaled him to her.

He leaped over the low embers and ran straight into Brenna's arms. They flared up in a brilliant burst of light, a star in nova, that singed the robes of the watching men. Then, in a moment, the firemaid and the charcoal burner were gone. All that was left was a pile of ashes that smoldered for years, sending up a pale blue spiral of smoke.

No one from the village was ever able to put it out.

THE
WIND CAP

There was once a lad who would be a sailor but his mother would not let him go to the sea.

"Tush, lad, what do you know of sailing?" she would say. "You are a farmer's son, and the grandson of a farmer. You know the turn of the seasons and the smell of the soil and the way to gentle a beast. You do not know the sea."

Now the boy, whose name was Jon, had always listened to his mother. Indeed, he knew no one else, for his father had died long ago. If his mother said he did not know the sea, then he believed he did not. So he went about his farm work with a heart that longed for sailing but he did not again mention the sea.

One day as he walked behind the plow, he all but ran over a

tiny green turtle on a clod of dirt. He picked the turtle up and set it on his head, where he knew the tiny creature would be safe.

When at last he was done with his plowing, Jon led the horse to pasture and then plucked the turtle from his head. To his surprise, he found it had turned into a tiny green fairy man that stood upon his palm and bowed.

"I thank you for your kindness," said the mannikin.

Jon bowed back but said nothing. For his mother had warned him that, when addressed by the fairies, it is best to be still.

"For saving my life, I will give you your heart's desire," said the green mannikin.

Still Jon was silent, but his heart sent out a glory to the sea.

The mannikin could read a heart as easily as a page of a book, so he said, "I see you wish to go sailing."

Jon's face answered for him, though his tongue did not.

"Since you put me on your head like a hat to keep me safe, I shall give you a different kind of cap in return, the kind that sailors most desire. A cap full o' wind. But this one warning: Never a human hand will ever be able to take it off."

Then with a wink and a blink, the fairy man was gone, leaving a striped cap behind.

Young Jon clapped the cap on his head and ran home to tell his mother.

When she heard Jon's story, his mother wept and cried and threw her apron up over her head, for a fairy gift is not altogether a blessing.

"No good will come of this wind cap," she said.

But the lad would have none of her cautions. The sailor's cap had bewitched him utterly. The very next day, without even saying farewell to his mother, he ran off to the sea.

Well, the wind cap worked as the fairy had said, and young Jon could summon breezes at will. But still there was that one condition: Never a human hand could take the cap off.

Now, that was bad and that was good. It was bad because Jon could not take his cap off before his captain nor could he take it off for bed. But it was also good. For neither could he lose the cap nor could it be stolen from him.

And since it was wind that sailors called for, and wind that Jon could supply, he soon was a most popular lad, although he had never before been away from shore. For if he twisted the cap to the right, he summoned the east wind. And if he twisted it to the left, he summoned the west. He could turn the cap to call both north and south winds and all the breezes between.

But if that was good, it was also bad. It was good because it made Jon a popular lad. But it was also bad. For once on board ship, he was not again let ashore. The captain would not part with such a prize.

For a year and a day, young Jon did not set foot on land. He saw neither the turn of the seasons nor the turning of the soil. Nothing but the churning of the waves. And there grew in his heart such a yearning to see the land, that it was soon too much for him to bear.

"Oh, let me go ashore just one day," he begged the captain when they had sighted land. "One day, and I swear I will return."

The captain did not answer.

"Just an hour," cried Jon.

But the captain was still.

"Then may you never see land again just as I cannot," shouted Jon.

The captain called his strongest men and they carried Jon belowdecks. And from that time on he was allowed up above neither night nor day, neither near shore nor on the deepest seas.

But Jon could not stop dreaming of the land. He even talked of it in his sleep. As much as he had once longed for sailing, he now longed for farming.

One quiet afternoon, when the sea was as calm and glassy as

a mirror and all the sky reflected in its blue, Jon lay fast asleep in his hammock in the hold. And he fell to dreaming again of the land. Only this dream was brighter and clearer than the others, for though he did not know it, the ship stood offshore from his old farm. In Jon's dream the seasons turned rapidly one into the next. And as each turned, so did Jon in his bed, and the cap on his head was twisted round and about, round and about, round and about again. It called up a squall from the clear sky that hit the ship without a warning.

The wind whirled about the boat from this side and that, ripping and fretting and gnawing the planks. It tore the sails and snapped the spars like kindling.

"It is *his* fault," the sailors cried, dragging Jon up from below. "He has called this wind upon us." And they fell upon Jon, one and another. They shouted their anger and fear. And they tried to rip the cap from his head.

Well, they could not take it from him, for it was a fairy cap. But they pulled it and twisted it one way and the next, and so the squall became a storm, the mightiest they had ever seen.

The ship's sides gave out a groan that was answered by the wind. And every plank and board shuddered.

Then the captain cried out above his terrified men. "Bring me that cap boy. I shall rid the ship of him." And when Jon

was brought before him, the captain grabbed him by the tail of his striped cap and twisted Jon three times and flung him far out to sea.

But the winds called up by the cap spun the ship those same three times around. It turned turtle, its hull to the sky, and sank to the bottom of the sea.

As Jon went under the waves, fingers of foam snatched off the cap. And as it came off, the storm stopped, the sea became calm, and Jon swam ashore. The cap followed in his wake.

When he got to land, Jon picked up the cap and tucked it into his shirt. Then, without a backward glance at the sea, he found his way home to his mother and his farm. He was a farmer's son, no doubt.

But in the winter, when the crops lay gathered in the barn and the snow lay heavy on the fields, he began to dream again of the sea. Of the sea when he had stood his watch and the world rocked endlessly and smelled of salt.

So Jon went to the wardrobe and got out the fairy cap and stood a long moment staring at it.

Then he tucked the cap into his shirt and went out to the field where he had found the fairy man. Looking up the field and down, over the furrows lined with snow, Jon smiled. He placed the wind cap under a stone where he knew the mannikin would find it. For magic is magic and not for men. Then he left again for the sea.

And this set the pattern of his days. For the rest of his life Jon spent half the year on a ship and half on the shore, 'til at last he owned his own boat and a hundred-acre farm besides. And he was known far and wide as Captain Turtle, for, as all his neighbors and shipmates knew, he was as much at home on the water as he was on the land.

THE WHITE SEAL MAID

On the North Sea shore there was a fisherman named Merdock who lived all alone. He had neither wife nor child, nor wanted one. At least that was what he told the other men with whom he fished the haaf-banks.

But truth was, Merdock was a lonely man, at ease only with the wind and waves. And each evening, when he left his companions, calling out "Fair Wind!", the sailor's leave, he knew they were going back to a warm hearth and a full bed while he went home to none. Secretly he longed for the same comfort.

One day it came to Merdock as if in a dream that he should leave off fishing that day and go down to the sea-ledge and hunt the seal. He had never done such a thing before, thinking it close to murder, for the seal had human eyes and cried with a baby's voice.

Yet though he had never done such a thing, there was such a longing within him that Merdock could not say no to it. And that longing was like a high sweet singing, a calling. He could not rid his mind of it. So he went.

Down by a gray rock he sat, a long sharpened stick by his side. He kept his eyes fixed out on the sea, where the white birds sat on the waves like foam.

He waited through sunrise and sunset and through the long, cold night, the singing in his head. Then, when the wind went down a bit, he saw a white seal coming far out in the sea, coming toward him, the moon riding on its shoulder.

Merdock could scarcely breathe as he watched the seal, so shining and white was its head. It swam swiftly to the sea-ledge and then with one quick push it was on land.

Merdock rose then in silence, the stick in his hand. He would have thrown it, too. But the white seal gave a sudden shudder and its skin sloughed off. It was a maiden cast in moonlight with the tide about her feet.

She stepped high out of her skin and her hair fell sleek and white about her shoulders and hid her breasts.

Merdock fell to his knees behind the rock and would have hidden his eyes, but her cold white beauty was too much for him. He could only stare. And if he made a noise then, she took no notice but turned her face to the sea and opened her arms up to the moon. Then she began to sway and call.

At first Merdock could not hear the words. Then he realized it was the very song he had heard in his head all that day:

> *"Come to the edge,*
> *Come down to the ledge*
> *Where the water laps the shore*

> *"Come to the strand,*
> *Seals to the sand,*
> *The watery time is o'er."*

When the song was done, she began it again. It was as if the whole beach, the whole cove, the whole world was nothing but that one song.

And as she sang, the water began to fill up with seals. Black seals and gray seals and seals of every kind. They swam to the shore at her call and sloughed off their skins. They were as young as the white seal maid, but none so beautiful in Merdock's eyes. They swayed and turned at her singing and joined their voices to hers. Faster and faster the seal maidens danced, in circles of twos and threes and fours. Only the white seal maid danced alone, in the center, surrounded by the castoff skins of her twirling sisters.

The moon remained high almost all the night, but at last it went down. At its setting, the seal maids stopped their singing, put on their skins again, one by one, went back into the sea again, one by one, and swam away. But the white seal maid did not go. She waited on the shore until the last of them was out of sight.

Then she turned to the watching man, as if she had always known he was there, hidden behind the gray rock. There was something strange, a kind of pleading, in her eyes.

Merdock read that pleading and thought he understood it. He ran over to where she stood, grabbed up her sealskin, and held it high overhead.

"Now you be mine," he said.

And she had to go with him, that was the way of it. For she was a selchie, one of the seal folk. And the old tales said it: The selchie maid without her skin was no more than a lass.

They were wed within the week, Merdock and the white seal maid, because he wanted it. So she nodded her head at the priest's bidding, though she said not a word.

And Merdock had no complaint of her, his "Sel" as he called her. No complaint except this: She would not go down to the sea. She would not go down by the shore where he had found her or down to the sand to see him in his boat, though often enough she would stare from the cottage door out past the cove's end where the inlet poured out into the great wide sea.

"Will you not walk down by the water's edge with me, Sel?" Merdock would ask each morning. "Or will you not come down to greet me when I return?"

She never answered him, either "Yea" or "Nay." Indeed, if he had not heard her singing that night on the ledge, he would have thought her mute. But she was a good wife, for all that, and did what he required. If she did not smile, she did not weep. She seemed, to Merdock, strangely content.

So Merdock hung the white sealskin up over the door where Sel could see it. He kept it there in case she should want to leave him, to don the skin and go. He could have hidden it or burned it, but he did not. He hoped the sight of it, so near and easy, would keep her with him. Would tell her, as he could not, how much he loved her. For he found he did love her, his seal wife. It was that simple. He loved her and did not want her to go, but he would not keep her past her willing it, so he hung the skin up over the door.

And then their sons were born. One a year, born at the ebbing of the tide. And Sel sang to them, one by one, long, longing wordless songs that carried the sound of the sea. But to Merdock she said nothing.

Seven sons they were, strong and silent, one born each year. They were born to the sea, born to swim, born to let the tide lap them head and shoulder. And though they had the dark eyes of the seal, and though they had the seal's longing for the sea, they were men and had men's names: James, John, Michael, George, William, Rob, and Tom. They helped their father fish the cove and bring home his catch from the sea.

It was seven years and seven years and seven years again that the seal wife lived with the man. The oldest of their sons was just coming to his twenty-first birthday, the youngest barely a man. It was a gray day, the wind scarce rising, that the boys all refused to go with Merdock when he called. They gave no reason but "Nay."

"Wife," Merdock called, his voice heavy and gray as the sky. "Wife, whose sons are these? How have you raised them that they say 'Nay' to their father when he calls?" It was ever his custom to talk to Sel as if she returned him words.

To his surprise, Sel turned to him and said, "Go. My sons be staying with me this day." It was the voice of the singer on the beach, musical and low. And the shock was so great that he went at once and did not look back.

He set his boat on the sea, the great boat that usually took several men to row it. He set it out himself and got it out into the cove, put the nets over, and never once heard when his sons called out to him as he went, "Father, Fair Wind!"

But after a bit the shock wore thin and he began to think about it. He became angry then, at his sons and at his wife, who had long plagued him with her silence. He pulled in the nets and pulled on the oars and started toward home. "I, too, can say 'Nay' to this sea," he said out loud as he rode the swells in.

The beach was cold and empty. Even the gulls were mute. "I do not like this," Merdock said. "It smells of a storm."

He beached the boat and walked home. The sky gathered in around him. At the cottage he hesitated but a moment, then pulled savagely on the door. He waited for the warmth to greet him. But the house was as empty and cold as the beach.

Merdock went into the house and stared at the hearth, black and silent. Then, fear riding in his heart, he turned slowly and looked over the door.

The sealskin was gone.

"Sel!" he cried then as he ran from the house, and he named

his sons in a great anguished cry as he ran. Down to the sea-ledge he went, calling their names like a prayer: "James, John, Michael, George, William, Rob, Tom!"

But they were gone.

The rocks were gray, as gray as the sky. At the water's edge was a pile of clothes that lay like discarded skins. Merdock stared out far across the cove and saw a seal herd swimming. Yet not a herd. A white seal and seven strong pups.

"Sel!" he cried again. "James, John, Michael, George, William, Rob, Tom!"

For a moment, the white seal turned her head, then she looked again to the open sea and barked out seven times. The wind carried the faint sounds back to the shore. Merdock heard, as if in a dream, the seven seal names she called. They seemed harsh and jangling to his ear.

Then the whole herd dove. When they came up again they were but eight dots strung along the horizon, lingering for a moment, then disappearing into the blue edge of sea.

Merdock recited the seven seal names to himself. And in that recitation was a song, a litany to the god of the seals. The names were no longer harsh, but right. And he remembered clearly again the moonlit night when the seals had danced upon the sand. Maidens all. Not a man or boy with them. And the white seal turning and choosing him, giving herself to him that he might give the seal people life.

His anger and sadness left him then. He turned once more to look at the sea and pictured his seven strong sons on their way.

He shouted their seal names to the wind. Then he added, under his breath, as if trying out a new tongue, "Fair Wind, my sons. Fair Wind."

THE
PROMISE

There were once fond and loving friends who were delivered of children on the same day and hour. They rejoiced in their good fortune and named the boy Kay and the girl Kaya, promising each other that the two children would never be parted. Indeed, they spoke often of that promise to the boy and girl. And the children, a laughing, talkative pair, took up the promise as their own and gave it freely one to the other.

But the fond friends died within days of one another, when the children were thirteen years old. The promise was not kept. Kay and Kaya were sent off to a distant city to live with their relatives, the boy to stay with an old uncle who was a sorcerer and the girl to a convent whose abbess was her aunt.

When they arrived at the city and stood hand in hand by the carriage, the old uncle looked them over and frowned. He pulled thoughtfully at the graying ends of his mustache, then dismissed the boy with a shrug. But the girl Kaya took his heart. He swore silently by the dark gods he worshipped that he would marry her when she came of age.

This decision the sorcerer did not speak at once, for he was used to a life built upon secrets which he rubbed to himself in the silence of his room 'til they festered like sores. Yet by the time he had delivered Kaya to the convent's care, he tumbled his secret into the air, for the girl's garrulous open nature had worked upon him and forced it out.

"I shall marry this girl, Sister," he said to the old abbess. "When she is sixteen I shall come for her."

Kaya shrank back from each syllable and her bright little face darkened. She began to tremble. "It is Kay I am to marry," she cried. "It was promised."

The sorcerer did not seem to hear. He spoke directly to the abbess. "Treat the girl well. I shall come for her. I swear it."

The abbess did not reply, for she was vowed to silence. But she held the trembling girl to her all the while the sorcerer was near. And when he had departed, dragging Kay after him, the abbess brought the girl into the convent and shut the gates after them with a mighty clang as if the noise alone could drive out demons.

The nuns went their silent ways, but Kaya wept. She had not their assurances. She alone among them had not been promised heaven. She played and read and sat wrapped in her own misery by the convent pool. Under the willow, with its green rosary of buds, where only the whisper of the water and tree disturbed the convent silence, Kaya grew into a woman. She could speak but she did not, except to the tree and the abbess' pool, for they alone returned her answers.

Now, though he had ignored it, the sorcerer had heard Kaya's cry. It shook his dark pride. And when he returned with Kay to their rooms, his heart was already hardened toward the boy, Kaya's promised one. Whereas he might have been a tolerant master, he was now a cruel one; whereas he might have pitied the boy's loneliness, now he felt no pity at all.

Kay bore it bravely for a long while—indeed he had no reason to do otherwise. He expected nothing from the old man and so he was not disappointed when nothing was his lot.

But at night, when the sorcerer was asleep, hands resting like withered leaves on his breast, the boy would lift the curtain of the single window in his room and look out at the glittering stars.

He would lean on his elbows and breathe half-remembered prayers whose words fell away from him with every passing day. As each word slipped away from memory, he substituted the one name he could recall: Kaya.

One night, when Kay was thus occupied, the old sorcerer awoke. The sounds of the boy's prayers were small daggers in his heart, for innocent prayer is the enemy of sorcery. He lifted himself from his bed and came silently to the boy's room.

There, elbows on the windowsill, Kay stuttered at the stars:

"And though I walk through . . .
The shadowed valley . . .
. . . I will not fear for . . .
. . . Oh, Kaya, Kaya . . . be with me."

"Kaya will never be with you," cried the old man, striking the boy with his hand.

As Kay cringed from the unexpected blow, the sorcerer moved his hand in a circle. "You *will* fear," he spat out. "And you will not pray. Indeed you will not say another word more." And he cast a spell on the boy.

Kay would have cried out then, more in anger than in fear, but he could not. His tongue cleaved to the roof of his mouth. His lips could not part. The sorcerer's magic had sealed them. He was as dumb as a beast.

"Go to bed," said the sorcerer, and turned in bleak triumph back to his own sleep.

But wordless, Kay was the enemy that, with words, he would never have been. He determined to resist the old man. Yet he was too young and too weak to fight the sorcerer outright. His resistance was a sly one. He began to undo the old man's long, tortuous spells. He dropped beakers in which potions were kept. He swept dust onto the pentagram on the floor. He ripped holes like mouse bites from the pages of the sorcerer's great books. And with each small act of resistance, Kay began to remember more words from his prayers until at last he could recall them all and repeat them in his head, though the words could not pass his mouth.

One evening, in the dead part of winter, Kay was ripping a snippet from *The Book of Night*. He used his nails, which had grown long and sharp in the sorcerer's service. Carefully he carved out a section in imitation of a mouse bite.

Suddenly the sorcerer swooped down on him as if from a great height.

"It is *you*. It has been you all this time, breaking my spells

and undoing my enchantments. Well, I will make an enchant-
ment you cannot break," the old man screamed.

The boy did not dare look at the sorcerer straight on, yet he
did not dare look away. He clouded his eyes over in order not
to see the old man clearly.

"All your defiances are for nothing," said the sorcerer. "You
are lost—and your Kaya is lost to you forever."

At Kaya's name, the boy leaped at the sorcerer's eyes and
would have found them with his nails if the old man had not
quickly spat out a spell:

> *"Beast to fish*
> *In virgin well,*
> *A kiss alone*
> *Can break the spell."*

At the words, Kay felt his bones shrinking, contracting, growing smaller and lighter. His arms clung to his sides. His feet
grew together. The air in his lungs was hot and seared his throat.
He tried to breathe and could not. He gasped and gasped, and
at each gasp the sorcerer laughed at him.

"You will leap upon no one again," the old man said. "Your
only leaping shall be done in a pool." He threw Kay, who was

now a silver carp, into a bucket of dirty water. Then, leaning over the bucket, where the fish swam around in maddened circles, the old man laughed again. "I shall show you your Kaya. You shall see her daily, and she you, but she will not be pleased with your appearance. A fish is the one pet the nuns are allowed. You shall be as chaste as they, and I shall have your Kaya."

The sorcerer lifted the bucket and put it by his bed, where he slept the rest of the night in dreamless sleep. In the morning he delivered the bucket with the silver carp to the convent with the admonition that none but Kaya should tend it.

The nun who took the fish in its bucket said nothing in thanks. Instead she went straight to the pool where Kaya sat wrapped in her own silences, her fingers idling in the water. The nun tapped the girl on the shoulder and Kaya looked up, her oval face framed by a halo of black hair.

Without further ceremony, the nun dumped the water-smooth silver fish into the pool. It circled once and came in under Kaya's fingers.

The girl was so frightened by this, she pulled her hand from the water and stared. At that, the fish gave a bubbling sigh and dove to the bottom of the pool. It did not come up again.

Kaya stood up and went inside.

But the next morning she was by the pool again. Sadness, like an old habit, claimed her. And when she put her fingers in the pool, drawing wavery pictures in the water, the great fish surfaced and circled them. And as he swam, the sunlight was caught in his scales and made iridescent patterns on the steep pool sides.

"What a strange and beautiful fish," said Kaya, trying out her words in the convent silence. "I wish you were mine, for I have no one at all."

At that, the carp circled under the green fingers of the willow tree and back again to the girl as if offering itself. And though she could not bear to feel its cold, scaly skin, Kaya fed the fish from her own fingers, dropping the crumbs of hard bread moments before the fish's mouth could touch her hands.

Less than a week later the old sorcerer came to the convent, and ordered Kaya brought to him. He stood, gnarled and frowning, in his black coat as the girl came to the door.

"It has been determined," he said, though he did not say by whom, "that tomorrow we shall be wed."

Kaya, who had not spoken to another human being since arriving at the convent, moved away from his words. She could find only one of her own in return.

"Kay," she said.

At the name, the sorcerer smiled, showing gray teeth beneath his mustache. "Kay cannot marry you."

"But we were promised to each other! Is he dead?"

The sorcerer's magic impelled him to the truth, but a strange truth, warped to his own purpose. "Not dead. But deeply changed, child. Changed beyond recognition. He does not want you as he is."

"He does not want me?"

"No."

Kaya began to weep and her old words tumbled between them. "I do not care. I want Kay. It was promised. It must be so."

The sorcerer was angry, but he could do no magic here, at the convent door. There was no way to stop the girl's tongue save in his own house in his own time.

"If Kay will not have me, no man will have me," said Kaya. "I shall become one of the nuns."

"You have been promised to me instead. I am to take Kay's place," said the old man, neglecting to mention that he himself was the one who had made the promise.

Kaya stopped crying. All her life she had been told about the power of promises. A promise given must be kept. She could not dismiss it lightly.

The sorcerer knew this. He saw his words working a subtle magic on Kaya's face. Seeing her consideration, he took it as acceptance. "The gift I sent, the carp. It should be nicely fatted by now. We shall have it today for our wedding feast."

Kaya looked clearly at the sorcerer for the first time. He stood before her playing idly with the iron button of his cloak. The threat behind his gentle tone was revealed by his casual cruelty to her fish. Suddenly she knew his promise for a lie. Still, she saw no way to escape him. So, to gain a little more time to think of a solution, she gave a lie in return.

"Tomorrow," she said.

"Tomorrow," said the old man, and left with a quick step.

Kaya waited until night, well past the hour of compline when the nuns spoke their last prayers in the candlelit chapel. Then, knowing the sisters were all asleep, Kaya rose and wrapped her cloak around her thin nightdress. She went out into the garden and stood by the abbess' pool.

"Fish," she called softly, "fish, come up."

The carp swam lazily to the surface. He never slept, but he lay for hours on the cool bottom of the pool. Although he was sleepless, he was not without dreams.

"*He* would marry me," said Kaya in a whisper. "*He* would

serve you for the wedding feast." And though she did not name the sorcerer in that holy place, the fish knew and shuddered.

"Do not fear, little friend," said the girl. "He shall have neither of us. I will drown you in the air and myself in the pool. This I promise. And we shall be together in Paradise."

She took off her cloak and laid it carefully under the tree, shivering slightly in the cool night air. Then she closed her eyes and reached for the fish that she had never dared touch before. It swam into her hands and lay there silently in her fingers. She pulled it out of the pool, and it neither gasped for air nor moved but shimmered silently in the moonlight.

"Ah, fish," said Kaya. "Would that I were your mate deep down in the abbess' pool." And she stroked the fish's damp head and, on a sudden notion, kissed it. "Farewell."

As she bent to put the fish on the cloak, it suddenly began to struggle and turn in her hands. She held it more firmly, but it kept struggling, and as it moved, it began to grow and change. Its scales sloughed off like little silver halos. Its tail cleaved in two. Its neck stretched and lengthened and on its head silken hair began to grow. It pulled free of her at last, a naked man.

Kaya leaped back and gave a little cry, and at her voice the sisters stirred in their cells and rose up by twos and threes. Kaya heard them coming to the convent garden, their steps sounding unnaturally loud in the stillness of the night.

Quickly Kaya bent down and picked up her cloak from beneath the tree and wrapped it around the man.

"Who are you?" she whispered, for his face was deep in the shadows.

But just as the nuns came to the garden, he turned his head and the moonlight fully lit his face.

"Kay!" she cried, and ran to his arms.

He smiled and embraced her but he said nothing in return. Though he was a man again, he still had no tongue to tell it.

A priest was summoned, and upon hearing their tale, married them at once by the pool with the old abbess nodding her agreement. So their promise was kept, and once they were joined in that holy place, the sorcerer and his magic could not come between them.

Kay never regained his speech. But Kaya, who had grown used to the wordless ways of the convent, was content. And the silence they shared throughout their long and loving life together was as variously shaded as speech.

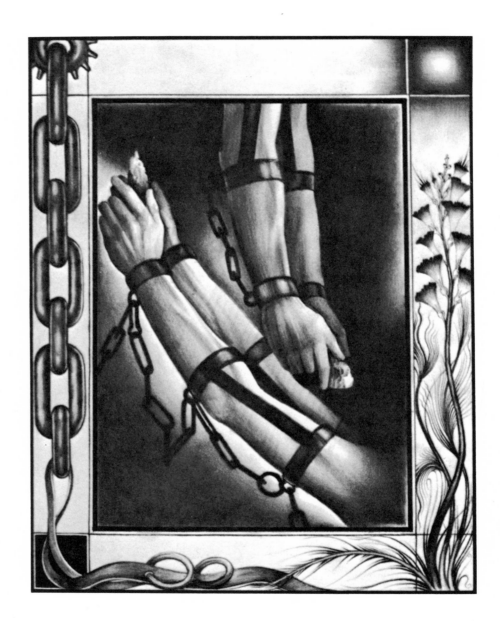

ONCE A
GOOD MAN

Once a good man lived at the foot of a mountain.

He helped those who needed it and those who did not.

And he never asked for a thing in return.

Now it happened that one day the Lord was looking over his records with his Chief Angel and came upon the Good Man's name.

"*That* is a good man," said the Lord. "What can we do to reward him? Go down and find out."

The Chief Angel, who was nibbling on a thin cracker, swallowed hastily and wiped her mouth with the edge of her robe.

"Done," she said.

So the Chief Angel flew down, the wind feathering her wings, and landed at the foot of the mountain.

"Come in," said the man, who was not surprised to see her. For in those days angels often walked on Earth. "Come in and drink some tea. You must be aweary of flying."

And indeed the angel was. So she went into the Good Man's house, folded her wings carefully so as not to knock the furniture about, and sat down for a cup of tea.

While they were drinking their tea, the angel said, "You have led such an exemplary life, the Lord of Hosts has decided to reward you. Is there anything in the world that you wish?"

The Good Man thought a bit. "Now that you mention it," he said, "there is one thing."

"Name it," said the angel. "To name it is to make it yours."

The Good Man looked slightly embarrassed. He leaned over the table and said quietly to the angel, "If only I could see both Heaven and Hell I would be completely happy."

The Chief Angel choked a bit, but she managed to smile nonetheless. "Done," she said, and finished her tea. Then she stood up, and held out her hand.

"Hold fast," she said. "And never lack courage."

So the Good Man held fast. But he kept his eyes closed all the way. And before he could open them again, the man and the angel had flown down, down, down past moles and molehills, past buried treasure, past coal in seams, past layer upon layer of the world, 'til they came at last to the entrance to Hell.

The Good Man felt a cool breeze upon his lids and opened his eyes.

"Welcome to Hell," said the Chief Angel.

The Good Man stood amazed. Instead of flames and fire, instead of mud and mire, he saw long sweeping green meadows edged around with trees. He saw long wooden tables piled high with food. He saw chickens and roasts, fruits and salads, sweetmeats and sweet breads, and goblets of wine.

Yet the people who sat at the table were thin and pale. They devoured the food only with their eyes.

"Angel, oh Angel," cried the Good Man, "why are they hungry? Why do they not eat?"

And at his voice, the people all set up a loud wail.

The Chief Angel signaled him closer.

And this is what he saw. The people of Hell were bound fast to their chairs with bands of steel. There were sleeves of steel from their wrists to their shoulders. And though the tables were piled high with food, the people were starving. There was no way they could bend their arms to lift the food to their mouths.

The Good Man wept and hid his face. "Enough!" he cried.

So the Chief Angel held out her hand. "Hold fast," she said. "And never lack courage."

So the Good Man held fast. But he kept his eyes closed all the way. And before he could open them again, the man and the angel had flown up, up, up past eagles in their eyries, past the plump clouds, past the streams of the sun, past layer upon layer of sky 'til they came at last to the entrance to Heaven.

The Good Man felt a warm breeze upon his lids and opened his eyes.

"Welcome to Heaven," said the Chief Angel.

The Good Man stood amazed. Instead of clouds and choirs, instead of robes and rainbows, he saw long sweeping green meadows edged around with trees. He saw long wooden tables piled high with food. He saw chickens and roasts, fruits and salads, sweetmeats and sweet breads, and goblets of wine.

But the people of Heaven were bound fast to their chairs with bands of steel. There were sleeves of steel from their wrists to their shoulders. There seemed no way they could bend their arms to lift the food to their mouths.

Yet these people were well fed. They laughed and talked and sang praises to their host, the Lord of Hosts.

"I do not understand," said the Good Man. "It is the same

as Hell, yet it is not the same. What is the difference?"

The Chief Angel signaled him closer.

And this is what he saw: Each person reached out with his steel-banded arm to take a piece of food from the plate. Then he reached over—and fed his neighbor.

When he saw this, the Good Man was completely happy.

THE LADY
AND
THE MERMAN

Once in a house overlooking the cold northern sea a baby was born. She was so plain, her father, a sea captain, remarked on it.

"She shall be a burden," he said. "She shall be on our hands forever." Then, without another glance at the child, he sailed off on his great ship.

His wife, who had longed to please him, was so hurt by his complaint that she soon died of it. Between one voyage and the next, she was gone.

When the captain came home and found this out, he was so enraged, he never spoke of his wife again. In this way he convinced himself that her loss was nothing.

But the girl lived and grew as if to spite her father. She

looked little like her dead mother but instead had the captain's face set round with mouse-brown curls. Yet as plain as her face was, her heart was not. She loved her father, but was not loved in return.

And still the captain remarked on her looks. He said at every meeting, "God must have wanted me cursed to give me such a child. No one will have her. She shall never be wed. She shall be with me forever." So he called her Borne, for she was his burden.

Borne grew into a lady, and only once gave a sign of this hurt.

"Father," she said one day when he was newly returned from the sea, "what can I do to heal this wound between us?"

He looked away from her, for he could not bear to see his own face mocked in hers, and spoke to the cold stone floor. "There is nothing between us, Daughter," he said. "But if there were, I would say *Salt for such wounds.*"

"Salt?" Borne asked, surprised for she knew the sting of it.

"A sailor's balm," he said. "The salt of tears or the salt of sweat or the final salt of the sea." Then he turned from her and was gone next day to the furthest port he knew of, and in this way he cleansed his heart.

After this, Borne never spoke again of the hurt. Instead, she carried it silently like a dagger inside. For the salt of tears did not salve her, so she turned instead to work. She baked bread in her ovens for the poor, she nursed the sick, she held the hands of the sea widows. But always, late in the evening, she walked on the shore looking and longing for a sight of her father's sail. Only, less and less often did he return from the sea.

One evening, tired from the work of the day, Borne felt faint as she walked on the strand. Finding a rock half in and half out of the water, she climbed upon it to rest. She spread her .skirts about her, and in the dusk they lay like great gray waves.

How long she sat there, still as the rock, she did not know. But a strange, pale moon came up. And as it rose, so too rose the little creatures of the deep. They leaped free for a moment of the pull of the tide. And last of all, up from the depths, came the merman.

He rose out of the crest of the wave, sea-foam crowning his green-black hair. His hands were raised high above him and the webbings of his fingers were as colorless as air. In the moon-light he seemed to stand upon his tail. Then, with a flick of it, he was gone, gone back to the deeps. He thought no one had remarked his dive.

But Borne had. So silent and still, she saw it all, his beauty and his power. She saw him and loved him, though she loved the fish half of him more. It was all she could dare.

She could not tell what she felt to a soul, for she had no one who cared about her feelings. Instead she forsook her work and walked by the sea both morning and night. Yet strange to say, she never once looked for her father's sail.

That is why her father returned one day without her knowing it. He watched her through slotted eyes as she paced the shore, for he would not look straight upon her. At last he went to her and said, "Be done with it. Whatever ails you, give it over." For even he could see *this* wound.

Borne looked up at him, her eyes shimmering with small seas. Grateful even for this attention, she answered, "Yes, Father, you are right. I must be done with it."

The captain turned and left her then, for his food was growing cold. But Borne went directly to the place where the waves were creeping onto the shore. She called out in a low voice, "Come up. Come up and be my love."

There was no answer except the shrieking laughter of the birds as they dove into the sea.

So she took a stick and wrote the same words upon the sand for the merman to see should he ever return. Only, as she watched, the creeping tide erased her words one by one by one. Soon there was nothing left of her cry on that shining strand.

So Borne sat herself down on the rock to weep. And each tear was an ocean.

But the words were not lost. Each syllable washed from the beach was carried below, down, down, down to the deeps of the cool, inviting sea. And there, below on his coral bed, the merman saw her words and came.

He was all day swimming up to her. He was half the night seeking that particular strand. But when he came, cresting the currents, he surfaced with a mighty splash below Borne's rock.

The moon shone down on the two, she a grave shadow perched upon a stone and he all motion and light.

Borne reached down with her white hands and he caught them in his. It was the only touch she could remember. She smiled to see the webs stretched taut between his fingers. He laughed to see hers webless, thin, and small. One great pull between them and he was up by her side. Even in the dark, she could see his eyes on her under the phosphorescence of his hair.

He sat all night by her. And Borne loved the man of him as well as the fish, then, for in the silent night it was all one.

Then, before the sun could rise, she dropped her hands on his chest. "Can you love me?" she dared to ask at last.

But the merman had no tongue to tell her above the waves. He could only speak below the water with his hands, a soft murmuration. So, wordlessly, he stared into her eyes and pointed to the sea.

Then, with the sun just rising beyond the rim of the world, he turned, dove arrow-slim into a wave, and was gone.

Gathering her skirts, now heavy with ocean spray and tears, Borne stood up. She cast but one glance at the shore and her father's house beyond. Then she dove after the merman into the sea.

The sea put bubble jewels in her hair and spread her skirts about her like a scallop shell. Tiny colored fish swam in between her fingers. The water cast her face in silver and all the sea was reflected in her eyes.

She was beautiful for the first time. And for the last.

ABOUT THE AUTHOR

Jane Yolen is known especially for her rare ability to create modern stories in the vein of the great classic folk tales. Her poetic prose has won her many awards and honors. Born in New York, she is a graduate of Smith College. She worked for a time as an editor of children's books before she decided to become a full-time writer. She is married and lives with her husband and their three small children in a lovely old house in Hatfield, Massachusetts. Among her many distinguished books are *The Girl Who Cried Flowers*, winner of the 1974 Golden Kite Award of the Society of Children's Book Writers, Finalist for the National Book Award, and an A.L.A. Notable Children's Book; and *The Moon Ribbon and Other Tales*, an Honor Book for the 1976 Golden Kite Award.

ABOUT THE ILLUSTRATOR

David Palladini was born in Italy, but came to the United States when he was very young and grew up in Highland Park, Illinois. He received his art training at Pratt Institute in Brooklyn. In addition to illustrating books, Mr. Palladini has received many awards and citations for his work in poster design and the graphic arts. Jane Yolen's *The Girl Who Cried Flowers*, which he illustrated, was chosen by the *New York Times* for its list of The Best Illustrated Books of 1974, and was selected by the American Institute of Graphic Arts for the Bratislava International Biennale (B.I.B.) 1975.